DESMOND COLE
GHOST PATROL

THE BUBBLE GUM BLOB

by **Andres Miedoso**
illustrated by **Victor Rivas**

LITTLE SIMON

New York   London   Toronto   Sydney   New Delhi

LITTLE SIMON

An imprint of Simon & Schuster Children's Publishing Division
1230 Avenue of the Americas, New York, New York 10020
First Little Simon paperback edition April 2022
Copyright © 2022 by Simon & Schuster, Inc.
Also available in a Little Simon hardcover edition.
All rights reserved, including the right of reproduction in whole or in part in any form.
LITTLE SIMON is a registered trademark of Simon & Schuster, Inc.,
and associated colophon is a trademark of Simon & Schuster, Inc.
For information about special discounts for bulk purchases, please contact
Simon & Schuster Special Sales at 1-866-506-1949 or business@simonandschuster.com.
The Simon & Schuster Speakers Bureau can bring authors to your live event. For more information
or to book an event contact the Simon & Schuster Speakers Bureau at 1-866-248-3049 or
visit our website at www.simonspeakers.com.
Designed by Steve Scott
Manufactured in the United States of America 0322 MTN
2 4 6 8 10 9 7 5 3 1
Library of Congress Cataloging-in-Publication Data
Names: Miedoso, Andres, author. | Rivas, Victor, illustrator.
Title: The bubble gum blob / by Andres Miedoso ; illustrated by Victor Rivas.
Description: First Little Simon paperback edition. | New York : Little Simon, [2022] |
Series: Desmond Cole Ghost Patrol ; 15 | Summary: Desmond and Andres
find themselves in a sticky situation when a new type of bubble gum
starts to consume Kersville—literally!
Identifiers: LCCN 2021027604 (print) | LCCN 2021027605 (ebook) |
ISBN 9781665914055 (pbk) |
ISBN 9781665914062 (hc) | ISBN 9781665914079 (ebook)
Subjects: CYAC: Chewing gum—Fiction. | Ghosts—Fiction. |
African Americans—Fiction. | Hispanic Americans—Fiction.
Classification: LCC PZ7.1.M518 Bu 2022(print) |
LCC PZ7.1.M518(ebook) | DDC [Fic]—dc23
LC record available at https://lccn.loc.gov/2021027604
LC ebook record available at https://lccn.loc.gov/2021027605

CONTENTS

Chapter One: Tall Candy Tales   1

Chapter Two: The Candy Kid   11

Chapter Three: Sweet Tooth, Sour Truth   19

Chapter Four: Not-So-Yum Gum   39

Chapter Five: You Don't Chew Me   57

Chapter Six: I CHEWS YOU   75

Chapter Seven: Sticky Stuck   83

Chapter Eight: The Ghost Plan   95

Chapter Nine: ABC   105

Chapter Ten: Bubble Burst   117

CHAPTER ONE

TALL CANDY TALES

Do you ever wonder why most grown-ups give kids such a hard time about eating candy? They have so many candy rules!

No junk food on school nights.
No sweets before breakfast.
No candy before bed.

Hmmm. I bet parents wait until we're asleep so they can stuff their faces with all the candy they want!

Not only that. Why do parents always tell us stories to scare us from eating too much candy?

Did you ever hear the story about the girl who ate so much taffy that her mouth got stuck together?

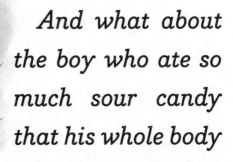

And what about the boy who ate so much sour candy that his whole body puckered until he disappeared? Poof!

Or the one about the kid who ate so many fizzy lava rocks that she erupted like a volcano?

Grown-ups never stop! They will tell you, *don't bite into jawbreakers, don't run with lollipops in your mouth, don't eat chocolate in swimming pools. . . .* Well, those rules actually make sense now that I think about it.

I've even heard a story about a girl whose mom was a dentist. And this girl's mom told her that eating candy was fine, but she had to brush her teeth as soon as she was done . . . *because of the tiny people who lived in her mouth.*

Her mom said the tiny people loved candy too. So, if any candy was left behind, they'd eat the candy . . . and her teeth! They wouldn't stop until every sweet tooth was gone!

I have to be honest: That story still makes me shudder. Plus, it reminds me to brush my teeth twice every day. Ugh.

My parents are cool about candy. They don't mind if I eat it . . . just as long as I give some to them. They call it "the Sweet Treat Tax." I have to give them a little piece of whatever I eat. Twenty percent to be exact. That's like a huge bite out of every candy bar!

But I don't mind—*usually*.

Halloween is different. Twenty percent of my candy haul is *a lot of candy*. And my parents are scientists, and they'll actually figure out exactly how much to take.

The Sweet Treat Tax is the worst! But there is one type of candy my parents can't stand: bubble gum.

Mom doesn't like the spit-covered bubbles. And the chewing sound drives Dad bonkers!

There is a rule in our house: no bubble gum allowed.

That's why I've never had bubble gum in my whole entire life . . . until I moved to Kersville, of course.

As a matter of fact, that's me, Andres Miedoso. I'm the one who's caught in that giant pile of pink, sticky stuff.

That's my best friend, Desmond Cole, swimming in that same pink, sticky stuff like a pro.

I bet you're wondering what that pink, sticky stuff is, right?

ANDRES MIEDOSO

It's a bubble gum blob.

And I bet you're wondering how we got ourselves into this situation.

Well, that's a long story. But we shouldn't start with the bubble gum blob. We should start with Marquis Chase, or as he's better known at Kersville Elementary, the Candy Kid.

DESMOND COLE

CHAPTER TWO

THE CANDY KID

I know what you're thinking. And no, Marquis wasn't a kid who was made of candy.

Kersville was a weird town, but it wasn't *that* weird!

No, Marquis was one of the nicest kids at school.

We called Marquis "the Candy Kid" because he was always selling candy to raise money for charity: chocolate bars for the Kersville Hospital, fruit chews for the baseball team, and gummy rings for the library. The Candy Kid had everything!

Marquis might have been even more popular than Desmond Cole. Well, at least until the bubble gum blob showed up.

But wait. I'm getting ahead of myself again. Where was I?

Oh yeah. I was telling you about Marquis.

Every day Marquis came to school
with a backpack of sweets. And this
was no ordinary backpack, let me
tell you. Not even close! This thing
was huge, and it had wheels like the
ones on a suitcase.

Throughout the day, Marquis stopped at every classroom to offer kids and teachers all kinds of candy treats they'd never heard of before.

There was candy from Japan, Iceland, Kenya, and just about everywhere else—talk about exciting! We were eating sweets from around the world!

Teachers and students couldn't get enough.

But let me tell you: Sometimes exciting new candy isn't as sweet as you think it's going to be.

Sometimes even sweets can turn out to be sour.

17

CHAPTER THREE

SWEET TOOTH, SOUR TRUTH

I remember the day it happened like it was just a few days ago.

Probably because it *was* just a few days ago!

Marquis brought a new kind of gum to school that no one had ever seen before.

"It's called Bubble Burst," he said, showing us the package it came in.

It had a rocket ship surrounded by fireworks on the label.

"That looks cool!" I said.

Marquis nodded. "And it tastes even better. The longer you chew this gum, the *more* flavorful it gets."

"That's hard to believe," Desmond said. "Most gum loses flavor when you chew it too long."

Marquis passed out sticks of gum to everyone—kids and teachers.

"This gum is different," he said. "I've been chewing on the same piece of gum for a week, and it tastes better than it did when I first popped it in my mouth."

Marquis handed me a piece of gum too. But I didn't try it like everyone else did.

"You'll love it," Marquis said. "The grape flavor gets grape-er, the cherry gets cherry-er, and the cinnamon gets cinnamon-er."

Cinnamon-er? I was starting to think the bubbles were making Marquis's brain a little too bubblier.

"Wow," Emily Jones said, her big eyes growing bigger. "This is the best gum I have ever tasted!"

Ralph Gomez sucked in his cheeks. "The sour apple is getting more and more sour."

"And the spicy is getting spicier and spicier . . . and *hot*!" Paul cried.

I swear I saw smoke come out of his mouth.

Soon everybody wanted to try Bubble Burst. Everyone except me. I just put the stick of gum Marquis gave me into my pocket.

"Are you sure you don't want to try it?" Desmond asked. "I think it's weird your parents never let you have gum before."

Desmond knew all about weird parents. Mr. and Mrs. Cole were always coming up with the weirdest (and grossest) meals you could think of. They cooked things like peanut-butter-and-marshmallow hamburgers or spaghetti with pickles and chocolate chips.

Let's not even talk about Mr. Cole's famous dessert: broccoli-flavored custard.

Here's some free advice: Never go to Desmond Cole's house for dinner. *Never.*

But back to that day at school. Bubble Burst was everywhere. Kids were blowing bubbles, and each one was bigger than the next. Students were chewing gum and making the loudest pops you'd ever heard.

The funny thing was that the teachers were doing the same! As a matter of fact, the gym teacher, Mr. Burpee, stretched his Bubble Burst gum into a long rope and started jumping with it. He looked so happy.

As soon as the kids saw what he had done, they started stretching their gum too. Some kids made lassos, and some made neck-laces and friendship bracelets.

Some kids created a climbing rope, and others played tug-of-war with their ropes.

I wish I could say this was the weirdest thing I'd ever seen since I'd moved to Kersville, but that wouldn't be true. This was kind of a normal school day in this town.

Kersville is a very, *very* unusual place to live!

As we rode our bikes home after school, Desmond asked me again, "Are you going to try Bubble Burst?"

He blew a bubble that was so big that he couldn't see where he was going. He swerved, missing a tree. Then the gum *bubble burst*, covering Desmond's whole face.

I laughed.

Bubble Burst gum looked like a lot of fun, but I still wasn't sure I wanted to try it. I didn't know why, but something told me to wait.

Right before bed that night, I took my stick of Bubble Burst from my pocket and put it on my desk. I needed to study it. I smelled it and squished it

and stretched it. I didn't understand
how something that looked so normal
could stay so flavorful and stretch so
much.

I yawned. This was a mystery I wasn't going to solve anytime soon.

So, I turned off my light and went to bed.

Of course, now I wish I had stayed up a little later. Maybe if I had, then the whole town wouldn't have been in so much danger.

If I had stayed awake a little longer, I would have seen that stick of Bubble Burst glowing bright in the dark. And I would have known for sure that Kersville was doomed!

CHAPTER FOUR

NOT-SO-YUM GUM

At school the next day, Bubble Burst was still on everyone's mind . . . and in everyone's mouth!

Some kids were still chewing the same piece of gum they'd started the day before.

Ewww.

The only person who wasn't as excited about Bubble Burst that day was Desmond Cole. As we watched everyone else chew, he whispered to me, "That gum is too good to be true."

"I know," I said, shaking my head. "There's something strange about gum that gets more flavor the longer you chew it."

Desmond got that look on his face, and I knew what he was going to say, even before he said it. "Bubble Burst gum must be haunted!" he told me.

"Haunted gum?" I asked. "That doesn't make any sense. Who would be afraid of gum?"

Other than me, of course.

"I'll prove it to you," Desmond said. "Come on."

Then he practically dragged me
down the hall and around the cor-
ner to the school library. Before we
walked inside, Desmond put his fingers to his lips and said, "Shhh."

We tiptoed past the head librarian, Mrs. Grumwald, who was sound asleep at the front desk. Her thick red glasses were on top of her head, and her mouth was wide open.

This was nothing new.

Mrs. Grumwald was always sleeping. Actually, none of the kids at Kersville Elementary had ever seen her awake! Some kids said she could break a world record for how long she could stay asleep!

The library was quiet except for Mrs. Grumwald's snores in the background. Desmond led me to the poetry section, which was all the way at the back of the library.

"Why are we here?" I whispered. "Is this the best time to stop and read poems?"

"Not exactly," Desmond said.

He reached up and pulled a red book from the middle of the bookshelf. And that was when the shelf slowly opened.

KLAK!

CRiiiiiiiiik...!

It was a secret door!

I wanted to shout "Cool!" But I didn't want to wake Mrs. Grumwald up, so I whispered it instead.

I followed Desmond inside, and the door closed behind us. The room was filled with science stuff. Desmond Cole had a laboratory!

I had a million questions. How long had he had this secret lab? How did he get all this equipment in here? Why was Desmond always so full of surprises?

I didn't ask any though because Desmond was in full Ghost Patrol mode.

He put on a white lab coat and reached for a microscope that was labeled GHOST CHECKER. He took out a stick of Bubble Burst and put the gum under the microscope, and he studied it closely.

GHOST CHECKER

That was when I heard a strange noise. It sounded like teeny-tiny paws.

Then I saw it: There was a gray rat next to the microscope, and it was sniffing the piece of Bubble Burst.

Oh no!

GHOST CHECKER

"Shoo! Shoo!" I said. I needed to get that rat away from the gum.

But Desmond looked up at me and said, "No, it's cool, Andres. This is Nibbles. He's my lab rat."

Lab rat?

Desmond turned to the rat and asked him, "Is this gum haunted, Nibbles?"

We watched as Nibbles sniffed the gum. Then he squeaked loudly and ran to a weird machine that looked like a tiny computer . . . a rat-size computer!

Then the computer spoke! "The gum appears to have ghost energy."

"I agree, Nibbles," Desmond said. "I knew it was haunted."

Desmond pulled out a cracker from his pocket and handed it to me. "Here, Andres. Why don't you feed him? Don't worry. He's friendly."

Nibbles hopped off the computer and grabbed the cracker from my hand. He held it in his tiny paws and munched on it, one little bite at a time.

I laughed. "So *that's* why you're named Nibbles!"

Desmond wasn't laughing with me. He was serious. "We have to go find Marquis fast," he said, putting the piece of gum back into his pocket. "I have a few questions for him."

"What's wrong?" I asked.

Desmond replied, "Let's just say that we've got a sticky problem on our hands!"

CHAPTER FIVE

YOU DON'T CHEW ME

Desmond and I found Marquis in the school courtyard, which was full of bushes trimmed to look like statues. Marquis was standing next to a dog-shaped bush.

We started to walk over to him, and then we saw the bush move.

It was time to hide and spy!

Desmond and I jumped into the nearest trash can. Not our best hiding spot—ugh.

We peeked out and saw that the dog-bush was actually a ghost!

And it was talking to Marquis. Then we saw the ghost give Marquis a big box of Bubble Burst gum!

"Thank you," Marquis said to the ghost. And he put the box into his backpack.

Then the ghost disappeared, and Marquis began walking, pulling his wheeled backpack behind him.

That's when I saw something really weird . . . even weird for Kersville. Something began to wiggle out of Desmond's pocket.

It was the piece of Bubble Burst . . . and it was getting bigger and bigger!

Desmond and I watched as the gum stretched and stretched until it reached the gum in Marquis's backpack. Soon, it became one long piece of gum-rope!

That was strange enough, but what happened next was unbelievable. The gum was so strong that it pulled Desmond and the trash can across the courtyard after Marquis.

"Wait, stop!" I screamed, but I was getting dragged too!

We trailed behind Marquis, all the way to the cafeteria. I was afraid we might get in trouble for dragging a trash can inside, but the cafeteria had way bigger problems.

Waaaay bigger!

The Bubble Burst had taken on a life of its own. Kids were running around and screaming, which really wasn't a good idea because the gum they were chewing was jumping

right out of their mouths and connecting to the gum in Marquis's backpack.

That was when things *really* got wild!

Blobs of Bubble Burst were every-where. Kids were tripping over smaller gum blobs. Other kids had sticky gum on their faces, in their hair, on their clothes. Everywhere!

And no matter how hard the kids pushed or pulled or yanked, they couldn't get free from the sticky clutches of the haunted gum!

Even teachers were in trouble!

Our music teacher, Mr. Timpani, yelled loudly when his hair got stuck in a big Bubble Burst blob. Then it lifted his hair off his head!

"Whoa!" I muttered to Desmond. "I didn't know Mr. Timpani wore a wig!"

"Me neither," Desmond replied. "Talk about a hairy problem!"

By then, the Bubble Burst blob was getting even bigger. It was connecting itself to all the other pieces of gum Marquis had given everyone, forming even longer ropes that reached out like creepy fingers!

"This thing is going to take over the whole school!" I cried.

"Watch out!" Desmond screamed. He shoved me out of the way as one of the bubble gum arms almost snatched me up!

We stood there and watched the Bubble Burst blob ooze its way out of the cafeteria.

"We have to follow it!" Desmond said.

I *knew* he was going to say that. And he was right. We had to do something.

If we didn't, the blob would take over all of Kersville!

The only problem was: How do you stop a giant bubble gum blob?

CHAPTER SIX

I CHEWS YOU

Here's a little bit of good news: Bubble gum blobs are really easy to follow for several reasons.

They are slow. Like super-duper slow. It wasn't hard to keep up with the blob at all.

They are bright. Like neon bright.

For some reason all the different flavors of gum mixed together and turned pink. That made it very easy to spot.

They leave a trail. A moist, gross path. Just thinking about the ooze it left behind makes me shudder!

They stay away from grown-ups. Well, except for teachers, that is. If there was a grown-up in the blob's path, it would go a different way. This was good because as Desmond and I followed the blob out of the school that day, we didn't have to worry about running into any adults. What would we say when they asked us why we weren't in school? Would they believe us when we told them we were saving the world?

But here's the bad news: The blob might not have cared about grown-ups, but it loved kids! In fact, it headed from the school straight to the playground!

And by the time it got there, school had already let out.

Kids were all over the place. They were sliding on slides, swinging on swings, and seesawing on seesaws. These weren't the kids from the cafeteria. They had no idea a giant bubble gum blob was coming their way!

"We have to warn them!" I told Desmond.

"I know," he said. "But what will we say? 'Watch out for the gum?'"

We thought about it and came up with a plan. It was something that would surely get the kids to run away.

"Bees!" we yelled. "Bees! Look out for the bees!"

Dear reader, if you learn only one thing from this story, let it be this: When a giant bubble gum blob is heading for a playground filled with kids, don't ever yell "Bees!"

It can only lead to a *bee*-saster!

CHAPTER SEVEN

STICKY STUCK

Everybody knows bumblebees are cool. The planet needs them. They make honey, which is yummy. Bees help gardens grow, and flowers are cool, I guess.

But bumblebees and kids are two things that should never mix!

When Desmond and I warned the kids to watch out for the bees, it worked . . . kind of. It got the kids to run away, but unfortunately, they ran right *into* the bubble gum blob!

Oh, it was the worst mess I'd ever seen . . . and I've seen a lot of messy messes since I moved to Kersville!

Kids were stuck *inside* the bubble gum blob! Desmond and I could see arms reaching out, faces peeking from the pink, sticky stuff, and guess what they were all yelling?

"Where are the bees?"

If an ooey-gooey blob ever attacks a playground near you, take my advice: Just yell "Watch out for the blob!" That might make more sense.

Desmond and I stood there and watched as the bubble gum blob just kept picking up everything in sight—barking dogs, cats lying out in the sun, even a whole car!

The blob was swallowing everything in its path!

We had to stop it!

"I have a plan!" Desmond said, snapping his fingers. He *always* had a plan.

He reached into his backpack and pulled out a tennis court net. "Here, tie this end to that tree, and I'll tie the other end."

When we had the net stretched across the playground and tied tight, Desmond yelled, "Hey, blob! Come over here!"

"W-what are you d-doing?" I asked, and I couldn't stop my voice from shaking. Why was Desmond calling the blob to us?

"Blob!" he called again. "Come and get more gum!"

The blob turned around way faster than either of us thought it could, and it started rolling our way.

"Get ready to run," Desmond told

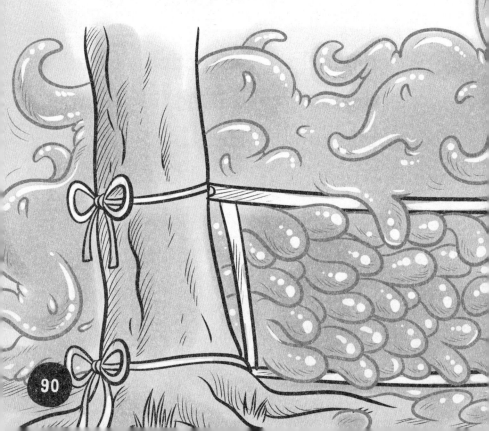

me. And when Desmond tells you to run, you do it!

The blob rolled up to the net, and guess what? It kept going . . . right through the holes.

"Oh no!" I screamed. "It's not working."

Then I realized what Desmond's plan really was.

When the blob went through the net, everything that was stuck in it got caught in the net.

All the kids and pets and cars were free. The blob just left them behind . . . which was good.

However, it kept on going *after us*, probably because Desmond told it we had more gum, which was bad.

Very, very bad.

CHAPTER EIGHT

THE GHOST PLAN

Where do you go when a giant bubble gum blob is chasing you? Home!

Desmond and I tumbled into my house, and we locked the front door behind us. Then I wondered if a bubble gum blob could actually blob up a whole house.

I hoped not.

That was when Zax, the ghost that lives with me, floated into the room.

"Thank ghost you're home!" he said. "Your mom and dad were doing some really long math problems, trying to stop a black hole or something. It was so boring without you."

"Shhh, Zax," I whispered while glancing out the window to see if the blob had followed us. "We're kind of busy."

"Busy with what?" he asked. "Is it fun? I hope it's fun. I want fun!"

Desmond turned to him. "It *is* fun," he said.

"No, it's not!" I told Zax. "We're hiding from the bubble gum blob!"

Zax floated over to the window and looked outside too. That's when we saw the pink ooze slowly coming down our street.

"Uh-oh," said Zax. "Somebody's been chewing Bubble Burst gum!"

"What?" I asked. "You've heard of this stuff before?"

"Of course. It's ghost gum," he said matter-of-factly.

"Tell us everything, Zax!" I practically begged. We needed to know what we were dealing with.

So Zax floated down closer to us and let us in on a little ghost secret.

"Ghosts have really, really bad breath," he whispered to us. "Here, let me show you."

He breathed on a plant and it shriveled up immediately.

"See?" Zax said. "It's horrible. That's why ghosts chew gum all the time—extra powerful gum. Plus, it's great for sharing."

Desmond asked, "What do you mean by sharing?"

"Oh, ghosts are big into sharing," Zax began. "If you see another ghost without any gum, you offer them a piece of yours . . . even if it means breaking off a piece of gum that you're already chewing."

Yuck! I thought I was going to faint right there!

But that didn't stop Zax from talking. "The great thing about Bubble Burst gum is that it's attracted to other gum," he continued. "It's kind of like a magnet. If you have one stick of gum, other pieces will find it. So you never run out, and you always have plenty to share!"

Well, now that we knew what the blob was, and why it kept getting bigger, all we had to do was figure out how to stop it.

No problem, right?

CHAPTER NINE

ABC

Kids have a word for gum that's already been chewed. We call it "ABC," as in Already Been Chewed. Get it?

But unlike ghosts, kids never ever share gum that's ABC with anyone else. We keep it to ourselves.

I mean, that's what I've heard. I've never chewed gum before, remember?

Still, I think everyone should keep their ABC gum to themselves. That's not too much to ask! But Desmond had a different idea. In fact, he had a plan.

And. It. Was. Gross!

"The bubble gum blob is making itself bigger and bigger so it can have enough to share with others," Desmond explained. "So the only way to stop it is . . . to eat it."

"Eat it?" I asked. "Some of that gum is ABC!"

Desmond turned to Zax. "We're going to need backup for this one. Can you get some of your ghost friends?"

"No problem," Zax said excitedly. "Ghosts love to help!"

And he floated through the wall, right out of the house.

Desmond and I reached out to everyone we knew from school and invited them over to my house. Pronto!

And the blob? Well, remember, it moved super-slow. It was still coming down the street, but we had time before it would reach my yard. And by the time it got here, we had an army of kids and ghosts just waiting to take a bite out of the blob.

Here's where the story started . . . with me taking the first jump into the bubble gum blob. Why did I go first? I don't know. Something came over me. I was supposed to wait until Desmond said "CHARGE!" But you might say I jumped the *gum*.

That's how I tried gum for the first time. And you know what? It was delicious!

Bite by bite, bit by bit, we ate that sticky pink blob until it got smaller and smaller and smaller.

The ghosts swooped in and ate from the top. The kids munched from the sides. And Desmond climbed a tree and dove into the middle so he could eat his way out.

Before long, all the Bubble Burst
was gone. The ghosts were happy.
The kids were happy. We had saved
Kersville!

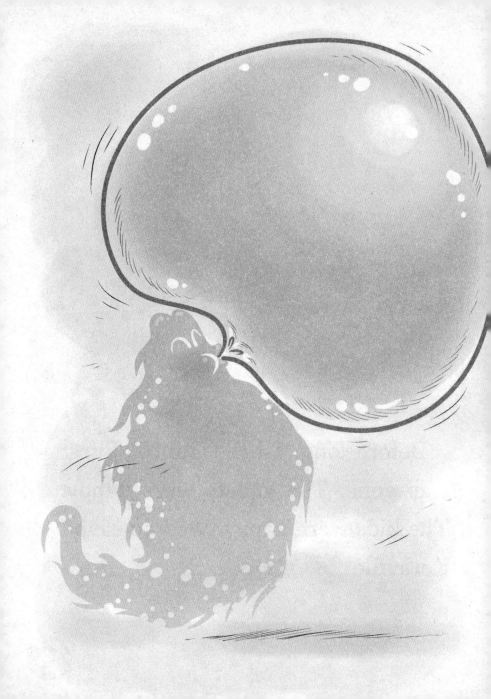

CHAPTER TEN

BUBBLE BURST

After everything that happened, Marquis doesn't sell Bubble Burst anymore.

Kids decided that most ghost candy is for ghosts only.

Most, but not all. Some ghost candy is great!

Luckily, we have Zax to teach us the ghost tricks from the ghost treats.

Like Zap Pops. You definitely don't want those. Trust me. Even ghosts are scared to try those. They are so hot and spicy that ghosts are afraid they will sizzle like bacon!

But Cider Spider Eggs are the best! They look like apples, but there's vanilla ice cream and apple pie inside. They're really cold when you hold them, but when you bite into one, it's warm and gooey.

Also, you need to know that the chocolate turtles for ghosts are totally different from chocolate turtles for humans. The same goes for lollipops,

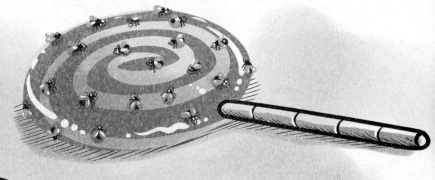

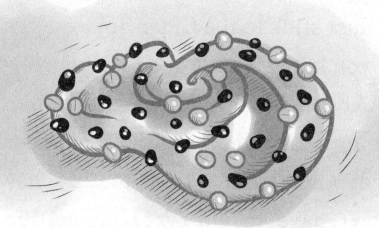

candy corn, and jelly beans. Ghost
jelly beans are just lima beans that
are left out in the sun until the juices
ooze out and turn brown. Ugh.

Just stick to the Cider Spider Eggs if you know what's good for you.

And here's a warning: If you're going to try ghost candy, remember that ghosts don't have teeth. They don't have to worry about getting cavities.

They never have to explain to *their* dentist what they've been eating.